JUNIOR BIOGRAPHIES

Kathy Furgang

ELON MUSK

ENTREPRENEUR

Enslow Publishing
101 W. 23rd Street
Suite 240
New York, NY 10011
USA

enslow.com

ambitious Having a strong urge to get ahead.

artificial intelligence Development of computers to do tasks that usually require a human.

electricity A type of energy.

engineer A person who designs, builds, or improves machines or systems.

entrepreneur A person who starts, organizes, or operates businesses by taking larger than normal risks.

extinct No longer living.

International Space Station A spacecraft for exploring and researching space.

renewable energy Energy sources that can be replaced easily, such as wind or sunlight.

CONTENTS

Elon Musk

CHAPTER 1
ELON AS A CHILD

An entrepreneur is a person who starts businesses by taking risks. It's a person who has good ideas that will hopefully pay off. Risks and good ideas have definitely paid off for one entrepreneur: Elon Musk.

Elon Reeve Musk was born on June 28, 1971, in Pretoria, South Africa. His mother, Maye, is from Canada. She was a model and dietician. His father, Errol, was an engineer. Elon has a younger brother named Kimbal and a younger sister named Tosca. When Elon was young, his parents divorced. His mother moved back to Canada. Elon lived with his father. They did not get along.

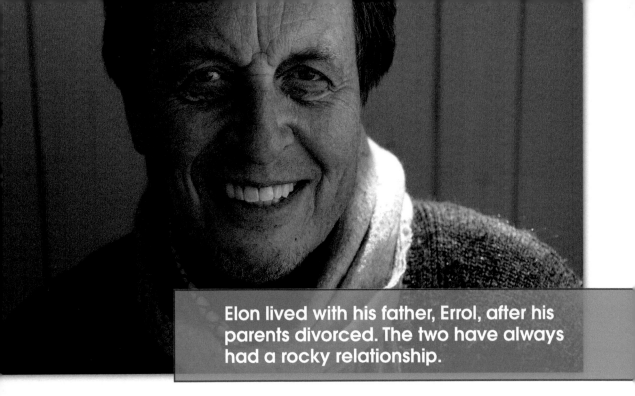

Elon lived with his father, Errol, after his parents divorced. The two have always had a rocky relationship.

LEARNING THE COMPUTER

Elon had a difficult time at school in South Africa. He was bullied by classmates. Once he was hurt so badly that he ended up in the hospital. One thing that helped Elon feel good growing up was the computer. When he was ten years old, Elon taught himself a computer language called BASIC.

Elon Says:

"I like video games. That's what got me into software engineering when I was a kid. I wanted to make money so I could buy a better computer to play better video games."

Elon grew up in Pretoria, one of the capitals of South Africa.

At sixteen, Elon and his brother tried to open a video game arcade near his high school. The city stopped the plan before the arcade opened.

AN EARLY PROJECT

Elon used his new knowledge of the computer language to create a video game. He called it *Blastar*. It was similar to the classic video game *Space Invaders*. After making the game, Elon sold it to a magazine for $500. He was only twelve years old at the time.

CHAPTER 2
AN ENTREPRENEUR'S SPIRIT

In South Africa, young people must train in the military. Elon wanted to avoid this. He wanted to live in the United States instead. Elon did some research. He found out that he could first move to Canada because his mother lived there. Then he could move to the United States. So at seventeen, he moved from South Africa to Canada.

Elon went to college in Canada. As planned, he then switched to a college in the United States. During these years he started to plan for a future in science, technology, and business.

Elon with his mother, Maye. She taught her children to be independent and work hard.

During school, Elon made extra money fixing and building students' computers in his dorm room.

STARTING OUT IN THE WORLD

After graduating from college, Elon moved to California. He wanted to make an impact on the world. He decided on three major areas where he wanted to make a difference. These areas were the internet, renewable energy, and space exploration.

Elon started his first successful company with his brother, Kimbal.

Elon started with the internet. In 1995, he worked with his brother, Kimbal, to start a software company. It provided maps to newspaper companies. After four years, the

Elon with Peter Thiel, the CEO of PayPal, in 2000

brothers sold the company for hundreds of millions of dollars. Elon used some of that money to start his next business. It was the first online money transfer company. This company, PayPal, is still popular today. When the company was sold in 2002, Elon made $165 million.

Elon Says:

"If something's important enough, you should try. Even if ... the probable outcome is failure."

CHAPTER 3
A REAL ENTREPRENEUR

By 2002, Elon had enough money to explore other business ideas. His next move was to start the space company SpaceX. The company was the first to launch rockets that could return to Earth and be reused. SpaceX's spacecraft bring supplies to the International Space Station.

SpaceX also plans to send people to Mars—for good. Elon believes humans need to learn to live on planets other than Earth. Many other species have become extinct because of conditions on Earth. He thinks this could happen to humans, too. One way to avoid this is by learning to live on another planet.

The SpaceX Falcon Heavy rocket is the most powerful rocket in the world.

Elon Says:

"When Henry Ford made cheap, reliable cars people said, 'Nah, what's wrong with a horse?' That was a huge bet he made, and it worked."

TESLA

In 2004, Elon started a car company, Tesla Motors. Since cars were invented, they have needed gasoline to run. The way that we make gasoline is harmful Earth. Cars from Tesla Motors are powered differently. They use electricity. Tesla cars travel much farther on one charge of electricity than cars travel on one tank of gasoline.

Tesla's first car was called the Roadster. It could go 250 miles (402 kilometers) on one charge of its electric battery. It could reach highway speeds in less than four seconds. Today, Tesla cars have improved even more since the first Roadster.

Elon poses with one of his Tesla Roadsters. The first Roadster was introduced in 2008.

Elon named his electric car company after Nikola Tesla. He was an inventor who lived in the late 1800s. Nikola Tesla played a large part in designing the electrical systems used today.

Elon arrives to speak at an event for the Boring Company in 2018.

THE BORING COMPANY

DIGGING TUNNELS

All of Elon's projects have been ambitious. Perhaps the most ambitious project is his plan to build tunnels underneath Los Angeles, California. He hopes that the tunnels will help traffic problems in the city. High-speed transportation systems would be built in the tunnels.

Elon has said that the project started as a joke, or a "hobby company." He named it the Boring Company because they *bore*, or drill, tunnels.

CHAPTER 4
COMPUTER SMARTS

Like most entrepreneurs, Elon Musk continues to come up with new ideas. In 2016, he joined a small group of people who started a computer company. Neuralink explores artificial intelligence. The company makes computers that could connect to the human brain.

As Neuralink's technology starts being used, it will help people with diseases or injuries of the brain. Over time, the company wants computers to connect to human brains. The goal is to make people more intelligent.

Artificial intelligence, or AI, is quickly becoming advanced. Many experts worry about AI. They feel it could end up harming humans instead of helping. Elon feels AI must be explored very carefully.

Elon speaks about Neuralink in 2015. He hopes the company will be able to help people with brain diseases.

THINKING INTO THE FUTURE

What does a successful entrepreneur hope to do in the future? Elon Musk never seems to run out of ideas. And his plans for his companies go way beyond just making new products. He hopes to change the way people think and live.

Elon believes in the goals of his companies. He wants all cars to be better for the earth. He wants space exploration to lead to colonizing, or building communities, on other planets.

Elon Says:

"Patience is a virtue, and I'm learning patience. It's a tough lesson."

In 2018, Elon attended an event where he answered questions about everything from cars to space exploration.

Elon Musk's work shows that humans must think about the future before it gets here. His ideas have already changed the way people think, work, and live. Only time will tell what impact his projects will have on our future.

TIMELINE

1971 Elon Musk is born June 28, in Pretoria, South Africa.

1988 Moves from South Africa to Canada.

1992 Starts attending the University of Pennsylvania.

1995 Starts a software company with his brother, Kimbal.

2002 PayPal is bought by Ebay, making Elon $165 million.

2002 Elon starts the space exploration company SpaceX.

2004 Starts the electric car company Tesla.

2016 The Boring Company begins drilling tunnels beneath Los Angeles, California.

2016 Elon helps start Neuralink, a company that makes AI brain technology.

BOOKS

Doeden, Matt. *SpaceX and Tesla Motors: Engineer Elon Musk.* New York, NY: Lerner, 2015.

Doudna, Kelly. *Automobiles: From Henry Ford to Elon Musk.* Edina, MN: Checkerboard Press, 2018.

Vance, Ashlee. *Elon Musk and the Quest for a Fantastic Future* (Young Readers Edition). New York, NY: HarperCollins, 2018.

WEBSITES

BrainPop: Engineering & Tech
www.brainpop.com/technology
Play games and learn about different inventions and innovations, including computer science and energy technology.

Kids Astronomy: SpaceX
kidsastronomy.com/space-exploration/spacex
Discover more about SpaceX and its goals for the future.

Smithsonian: Early Cars
www.si.edu/spotlight/early-cars
Read more about cars and the history of the automobile.

INDEX

Published in 2020 by Enslow Publishing, LLC.
101 W. 23rd Street, Suite 240, New York, NY 10011

Library of Congress Cataloging-in-Publication Data
Names: Furgang, Kathy, author.
Title: Elon Musk : entrepreneur / Kathy Furgang.
Description: New York : Enslow Publishing, 2020 | Series: Junior biographies | Includes bibliographical references and index. | Audience: Grades 3-5.
Identifiers: LCCN 2018050166| ISBN 9781978507913 (library bound) | ISBN 9781978508927 (pbk.) | ISBN 9781978508934 (6 pack)
Subjects: LCSH: Musk, Elon—Juvenile literature. | Businesspeople—United States—Biography—Juvenile literature. | Businesspeople—South Africa—Biography—Juvenile literature.
Classification: LCC HC102.5.M88 F87 2020 | DDC 338.092 [B] —dc23
LC record available at https://lccn.loc.gov/2018050166

Printed in the United States of America

To Our Readers: We have done our best to make sure all website addresses in this book were active and appropriate when we went to press. However, the author and the publisher have no control over and assume no liability for the material available on those websites or on any websites they may link to. Any comments or suggestions can be sent by e-mail to customerservice@enslow.com.

Photos Credits: Cover, p. 1 Pascal Le Segretain/Getty Images; p. 4 Gregg DeGuire/WireImage/Getty Images; p. 6 Cyrus McCrimmon/Denver Post/Getty Images; p. 7 Alexandre G. Rosa/Shutterstock.com; p. 9 JB Lacroix/WireImage/Getty Images; p. 10 Neilson Barnard/Getty Images; pp. 11, 19 © AP Images; p. 13 Joe Raedle/Getty Images; p. 15 Nick Zonna/Splash News/Newscom; p. 16 Lucy Nicholson/REUTERS/Newscom; p. 21 Diego Donamaria/Getty Images; interior page bottoms (business icons) Dmitriy Domino/Shutterstock.com.